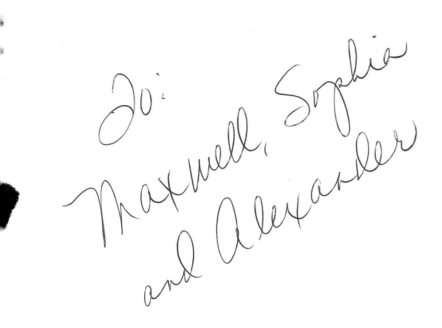

To:
Maxwell, Sophia
and Alexander

Love,
Debbie
Bronson

#6 in the "Animalopolis" Series

2 Books in 1:
"Elliott Saves the Day for Frieda"
&
"Gaffy's Tournament"

Serendipity Publishing
Germantown, Tennessee
Serendipitypub@AOL.com

Other books in the "Animalopolis" Series include:

"Animalopolis A to Z"
 www.createspace.com/3338488
"Bailey the Beaver's Bell Won't Ring"
 www.createspace.com/3333773
"Carlos the Cat Gets Lost"
 www.createspace.com/3342851
"Denver Loses His Checkerboard"
 www.createspace.com/3343251
"The Adventures of Elliott, Frieda & Gaffy
 www.createspace.com/3341411

All books in the series can be found at Amazon.com

The Adventures of Elliott, Frieda & Gaffy

Written by Debbie Bronson
Illustrated by
Tammy Hill & Debbie Bronson

Elliott Saves the Day

for Frieda

Written by Debbie Bronson
Illustrated by
Tammy Hill & Debbie Bronson

Frieda the Fox

is as sly as can be.

When the lights went out,

though, Frieda could not see.

She was trying to read

to the kindergarten class.

She was hoping the outage

would hurry and pass.

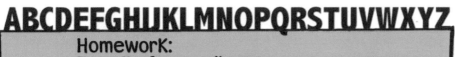

ABCDEFGHIJKLMNOPQRSTUVWXYZ

Homework:
Eat all of your dinner
Brush your teeth before bed
Don't talk back to your Mother
Be at school on time tomorrow

ABCDEFGHIJKLMNOPQRSTUVWXYZ

Class Work:

Please try not to cry

But, the kids were bored

and began to cry.

"Oh, what can I do?",

Frieda said with a sigh.

She thought and she thought

and was usually quite clever.

But, this time the lights

seemed to stay out forever.

Suddenly an idea came to

Frieda that day.

Her friend Elliott Eel

had an electric sashay.

Elliott was swimming

around in his tank,

not a care in the world,

he thought, as he sank.

Elliott truly was

really quite bored.

He'd already played

with the ball he adored.

So, when Frieda called out

to ask him for help.

Elliott yelled, "Sure I can",

with a yelp.

Frieda hoped that her plan

would work out OK.

Holding hands down the hall

went the class that day.

They found Elliott's tank

in the hall by the gym.

All of the kids

really were taken by him.

Elliott Eel would

flip his tail

and electric lights

would shoot out without fail.

Frieda used the light

from Elliott's flipping

to finish the story

without once ever tripping.

The lights came back on

by the end of the day.

But, the kids would never

forget Elliott's sashay.

Elliott Eel was happy that night.

He had helped out a friend

and that felt so right.

While Frieda had learned that

no matter how sly,

we all need good friends

to help us get by.

Gaffy Giraffe's Tournament

Written by Debbie Bronson

Ilustrations by
Tammy Hill & Debbie Bronson

Gaffy Giraffe,

whose neck was so long,

excelled when he played

a game called ping pong.

While Tyler the Turtle,

whose legs were so short,

got stuck in his shell

while playing the sport.

Now Gaffy beat Tyler

quite smartly, it's true.

But, up next to play

was a chimp from the zoo.

The chimp's name was Charlie

and he was quite good.

His chances were slim,

the chimp understood.

Gaffy and Charlie

played such a good match

ideas of a tournament

started to hatch.

The animals lined up

to sign up to play

and after much chatter

selected a day.

The tournament started

without even a kink.

A tiger named Thomas

played a leopard named Link.

At the end of the match

Thomas won 3 to 2

and the leopard named Link

headed back to the zoo.

Next up to the table

was a penguin named Paul

and a beautiful peacock

whose feathers stood tall.

The peacock named Patty

played well on her side.

Then she strutted on over,

her feathers fanned wide.

Finally the time came for Gaffy to play.

His long giraffe neck

made him swagger and sway.

Charlie the chimp on the other side stood

with his very best paddle

and looking so good.

Gaffy and Charlie then started to play.

They played and they played

and they played all day.

At the end of the day

they were tied 2 to 2.

And they started to wander

if they'd ever be through.

Charlie the Chimp

jumped around with his paddle.

While Gaffy on his side

put up a great battle.

They pinged and they ponged,

but no one could score.

Then Gaffy and Charlie

both fell to the floor.

Penelope Poodle

and Carlos the Cat

both jumped from their seats

with wonder at that.

Gaffy's long neck was

really quite sore

as it stretched across the table

and down to the floor.

Gaffy and Charlie

had played a great game.

But, when they collapsed

their scores were the same.

Then at the same time

they both started to laugh.

There was nothing so funny

as a worn out giraffe.

They lay there exhausted

and too tired to think.

Then Gaffy looked over

and gave Charlie a wink.

Gaffy told Charlie

with his widest grin.

"You know, sometimes

it's just not important to win" !!

Made in the USA